The Beggar's Knife

THE BEGGAR'S KNIFE

Rodrigo Rey Rosa

Translated by Paul Bowles

City Lights Books
San Francisco

Cover photo by Chris Felver
Drawing by Maria M. Rey Rosa
Photo of Rodrigo Rey Rosa by Paul Bowles

These stories were originally published in:
"The Monastery," *El Imparcial* (Guatemala)
"The Path Doubles Back," Red Ozier Press (New York)
"The Rain and Other Children," *Frank Magazine* (Paris)
"The Release" & "The River Bed," *The Threepenny Review*
     (Berkeley, CA)

Library of Congress Cataloging in Publication Data

Rey Rosa, Rodrigo, 1958-
    The beggar's knife.

    I. Title.
PQ7499.2.R38B4   1985   863   85-5742
ISBN 0-87286-166-X
ISBN 0-87286-164-3

City Lights Books are edited by Lawrence Ferlinghetti
& Nancy J. Peters and published at the City Lights Bookstore,
261 Columbus Avenue, San Francisco, California 94133

CONTENTS

THE RELEASE

The light in the room was on. It was half past
four on a December morning. A voice from outside
awoke him: an old friend of his father's. "They've
called. You're supposed to go to the Plaza de Tecún."
Without answering, he sat up in the bed, passed his
hand over his face and hair, and then lay down again,
remaining immobile, his eyes fixed on the ceiling.
Soon, becoming fully conscious, he sprang up; he
had his clothes on. He checked his wallet and stooped
over to reach something under the bed: a black duffel
bag. He tested its weight and slung it over his shoulder. Turning off the light, he went out and down the
stairs that smelled of recently waxed wood. He
stepped through an antechamber and across a corridor. The other man was waiting for him outside the
entrance door; his smile of sympathy went unnoticed
by the man he had come to awaken, who pushed by,
paying him no attention. "Like a sleepwalker,"
thought the other. There was a grey automobile in
the garage. The man put the bag into the trunk, got
into the driver's seat, and moved off.

The streets were empty. He noticed that it had
rained, and saw the familiar reflections of the red and
green lights on the wet asphalt; he realized that he
was shivering with cold. "The Plaza de Tecún," he

said to himself, and smiled mechanically. "Why does it seem so funny?" Rather than looking for an explanation he made himself concentrate on the present moment. Soon he turned into a brightly lighted avenue; now that he had it all to himself, he thought of it as an enormous tunnel. He felt no anxiety; what he was doing had been ordained by a power that was not to be questioned. It was one of those things "more important than life itself."

The way to the Plaza de Tecún was enjoyable in a sense: there was silence all around, and he had managed to keep his thoughts at bay. It was as if he were reliving a night from long ago; he observed himself watching a ritual, innocently and with a kind of dread. When he got to the plaza he was impressed by the silhouette of the statue. Taking his time, he parked the car and then turned on a flashlight. He walked over to the pedestal and noticed that rust covered the statue's gigantic feet, as well as the lance it carried. On the ground there was a stone about the size of a clenched fist, and under it a piece of white paper. He lifted the stone and removed the paper. Back in the car he hastily unfolded it. Reading the words written there was like pronouncing a formula. (The immediate future and the immediate past were needles piercing the artificial bubble of the present moment.) "Drive at 50 kilometers per hour. Lower all four windows. Follow the red line shown on the map." Upon ceasing to analyze his reactions he had managed to avoid considering what these people might be like, these who held his fate in their hands, but now his reflections included the presence of a human volition; he began to see its features. He studied the map. The red line led along a narrow street giving onto the plaza. After he had put the windows down, he drove on.

As he moved along the street his feeling of revulsion grew; the channels of his memory filled again. Even though the circumstances still seemed extraordinary, he was beginning to feel that he was carrying out a routine action. The line designating the route he was to take finally turned into the street that led to the market. He was obliged to drive very slowly: men carrying sacks and cartons were crossing the street in leisurely fashion. They seemed to be moving with their eyes shut. He looked again at the map, and parked in front of a fruit stand. From behind a pile of white barrels that stood on the sidewalk a man emerged and signaled to him. He opened the rear door of the car, and the stranger, followed by two other men, got in. They did not speak. He was pale and still shivering with cold. "Where to?" he asked. "Straight ahead! Straight ahead!" ordered a voice behind him.

The sun had not risen but it was already light. As they went along, the street had fewer people in it. "Drive faster," they told him. They crossed the city, going northward. He drove calmly, noticing everything as he went past. He saw the doors and windows and walls, and then the orchards and the countryside to the left and right of the road, but nothing stayed in his mind. He imagined a man with the stripe of the map's red line running across him. It was like a vision produced by a magician, and then unexpectedly it was gone. "We've come a long way from the city," he thought.

One of the men said: "Stop under those pine trees," and pointed to the right. He had to put on the brakes with great force. Then he realized that a white car was coming toward them; it stopped beside them. They told him to get out, and pushed him into the other automobile. Four hands held his arms while someone fitted blacked-out goggles over his eyes. He heard a hoarse voice say: "Right. It's the cash." There was the explosive sound of the trunk being slammed shut. Tires squealed, and he understood that his own car was being driven on. "They've got what they wanted," he thought. "Why are they doing this to me?" Then slowly the car he was in began to move. "What's happening?" he asked. The reply was a vicious blow in the region of his liver. He felt nausea and tried to lean forward, but they held him fast. He vomited a little saliva and some yellowish liquid. Then he smelled alcohol, and felt a cold friction on the nape of his neck. "We're going to put you to sleep," they told him, and the needle as it went in startled him. "You're going to kill me," he said aloud. His sight clouded over, a buzzing sound increased. He wanted to speak, and found that he could not produce a word. The two men beside him put him at their feet and covered him with a green blanket. His cheek bumped against the floor and the vibration of the motor stupefied him. He noticed that his breathing was becoming weaker; inside him was the thought: "I'm dying." His eyes were open, but nothing was real. "Where will they take me," he asked himself, "since now there's no need for me to go anywhere?"

They drove to the city, through one of the principal streets, went around two or three corners, and turned in at a house with a large and well-tended garden. Three men carried him into the house. They took him down to an underground room, where there was a canvas cot. A pail of water stood on the floor, and a pile of books. They laid him out on the cot, and one of them, the youngest, sat down on a chair by the door. The others went out and bolted the door from outside.

He remained unconscious for a long time. Then he raised his eyelids and moved his eyes slowly. "This is Hell," he said to himself, and the thought resounded within him, but with increasing feebleness. He tried to move his hand and was not able to; it seemed to him that his heart waited a long time between each beat. He could not form another sentence in his mind. Unrelated ideas appeared and disappeared one after the other.

It was already night when someone came running down the stairs into the cellar, knocked twice on the door, slid open the bolt, and came in. "They caught them. With the cash," he said to the guard who had been sitting by the door. "We've got to get him out of here." Between the two, they lifted him off the cot and carried him up to the garage, where they put him again into the car. They drove out into the street, carefully crossed the city, and took the western road out. After they had driven for a few minutes, they parked along a wide curve, pulled him out and placed him face-down on the pavement. The young man crouched down beside him and said: "I'd say he's already dead." He pulled a revolver from his belt and fired it absently into the body. There was lightning in the north.

Later, when he opened his eyes, the intense light dazzled him. He stared this way and that, and found that the walls revolved. A woman in yellow approached, took his hand, leaned over him and moved her fingers lightly over his hair. Her lips formed words but he could not hear her. He looked into her eyes, and it seemed to him that they were empty sockets. "They're pretty," he thought, and tried to tell her, but no word came out. The woman put her fingers on his eyelids and pressed them shut. She caressed his face and the backs of his hands, and moved away. Something cracked in his thorax. A voice asked him: "Are you asleep?" In his mind he said yes. But to himself he said: "I'm wide awake." "Do you know who I am?" the same voice went on. He did not try to answer, but he understood that it was his wife. They had let her go. Then he felt another blow: a faint sound. "It's my heart," he thought, and inside himself: "*It's enough. Let it stop.*" He died then.

For my parents

THE SIGN

The first time it happened to me was in T . . . , which is considered a mysterious city both by those who do not know it and by those who do. I woke up in the morning, and looking into the worn-out bathroom mirror on the upper floor of the Villa Sadi-Sahda, I noticed a scratch on my face. I thought a moment, but could not recall having hurt myself the previous evening; if I had done it during a dream in the night, I had completely forgotten the dream. It was two days before the scab had disappeared from my cheek.

The second time, seven nights afterward, I was in the town of M . . . I awoke with a similar scratch, and without the faintest memory of any accident or dream which might explain it. But this time, perhaps impelled by the strange sensation the sight of the second scratch produced in me, I determined to find the cause and to learn how such a mark might have been made.

I began by imagining that in the midst of a possible nightmare I might have clawed myself. But it struck me as unlikely that I should have managed twice to inflict the identical scratch: a line beginning just below the center of my eye and cutting deeper as it described a half-moon that ended near the corner of my mouth. Disfigured in this way, I found it embarrassing to have to speak to anyone, even someone I did not know.

During the voyage between M . . . and G . . . I decided to mention my problem to an old friend of mine. When I had told him my story, he smiled. Nevertheless, he agreed to spend the following nights with me and keep an eye on me as I slept. Nine nights he stayed by my side without noticing anything extraordinary. But the morning after the first night I spent by myself, the scratch appeared again. So I went to his house to show it to him. After examining it, he agreed to return and watch my sleep again. He made himself comfortable in the adjoining room, and had me make a tiny hole in the connecting wall so that, as he explained, he would be able to observe me without his presence affecting possible subconscious activity during my sleep. For twenty-seven fruitless nights he watched me steadfastly, and at the end of that time we agreed that the thing was beyond us. But again, on the second night I passed by myself, the scratch was repeated, although this time with a variation: instead of the descending curve, it was an inverted letter U, just below my eye.

It had become clear that a second person, even if hidden, would prevent the inexplicable design from being marked on my face; thus I abandoned the idea of seeking outside help. I did not go out of the house that day; I did not want anyone to see me, and I shut myself into the small room I used as a study, determined to solve the puzzle. I knew only one thing: I must find the answer by myself.

It would be tedious to recount the various devices I conceived in order to observe myself while I slept; I admit that the idea itself was absurd and that the abstract search I was engaged in was so monotonous that I was overcome by sleep as I leaned over my desk. What I dreamed was simply a prolongation of the state of siege resulting from my obsession. In the bathroom there was a circular mirror, and I dreamed that I removed it from the wall and carried it into my bedroom. I took several books from the shelf and made a pillar against which I leaned the mirror in such a way that when I was lying in the bed I could see the reflection of my entire body. Then I took two tweezers from a little box, and somehow affixed them to my eyelids in such a way that it was impossible for me to shut my eyes. I remained asleep with my eyes open, and watched myself in the slanting mirror. I heard then what sounded like the fluttering of wings. What came to strike my face was something without a clearly defined shape, like a little cloud with claws. It opened its black bill, and I made a vain effort to shut my eyelids. It was then, made desperate by my helplessness, that I awoke. As I reconstructed the dream I felt my fear leaving me.

Later in the night, resting on my bed, feeling that by doing this I was ending the mystery, I began to write this deformed account. And, in spite of that, two mornings later, there was the mark, now unexpected, of an inverted letter U under my eye.

THE PATH DOUBLES BACK

ONE

He went slowly down the path. A sick man lay on the ground, his eyes rolled back, his skin colorless, selling agony in his outstretched hand. Before he reached the house he had to get past two lost-looking dogs and a dead rat.

Although the door was shut, he was sure there was a fire in the fireplace. Someone was coming along the path he had taken. For an instant he failed to recognize the door and the iron grillwork, but then they returned to looking as they had. He peered at the ground, perhaps in search of a note, an explanation. Then he turned to look back at the hill, with some curiosity and a little fear, hoping to see the face of the person following him.

He put his hands into his pockets as if he had forgotten something, and realized that they were empty. He scratched the cloth and stood as straight as possible.

The other man was taller than he. He walked with his arms folded behind his back, one step here and one step there in his bare feet. When he got to the stone steps he stood still, deliberately barring the way.

Without speaking, the first man started back down the steps. The second did not move until their two bodies were almost touching. Then, frowning, he let the other by. He climbed the three steps. The beating of his heart surprised him. Without moving his feet he turned his head.

The stranger was running.

The three lines in his forehead were more visible. He took two long steps and touched the door.

Once again he looked out at the path; it was empty.

He took out a key and put his ear close to the door, listening in vain for some sound. Slowly he fitted the key into the door, gave it two turns, and pushed.

There was light in one of the rooms. The fire had been neglected, and was about to go out. The light came from the end of the corridor. Without making any sound, without touching anything, he made his way to the last room. Fortunately, it was empty. The entire house was empty.

The man had sat down by the fire. His forehead showed preoccupation and the presence of many ideas.

After half an hour his expression changed suddenly at the sound of three short raps on the door. He felt guilty. Not to have been able to ask anything of the stranger! His surprise had been too great. Even so, he felt like a coward.

He opened the door.

First the wind entered, compact and cold. In place of seeing the expected smile, and without feeling any pain, he was stabbed. The blade opened the flesh at the navel and swept upward, leaving a red furrow, almost to the throat. Outside, the stars flared. The sky tore in half before his eyes as he fell. For a long time he went on falling. The house began to change into a cloud and then to be moving farther away; the hill opposite became a wave; the steps were an elephant, and the path an invisible tunnel.

He no longer felt the wind's chill, and the forms of things ceased to trouble him as they took on ever deepening shades of blue.

When he realized that air was no longer passing through his nostrils he understood that he had no nose.

When he had searched insistently through his memory, he recalled that he was swimming. He also recalled the stranger and the invisible tunnel. Full of thoughts, he swam ahead.

TWO

The first two male children to be able both to speak and to walk are set apart from the others. An old man takes them to the temple, where they are brought up to go naked, remaining thus unclothed until they have been introduced to all the arts and games, and until they have read all the books.

At the age when they are taught about light, one of them is led to the interior of the temple, and there, through a curtain of fine red sand, he sees wine and women for the first time. And at the hour when the moon makes sleep the most profound, someone (thin and old) approaches the chosen one, and while he sleeps, puts a black flower into his mouth, rubbing its pollen over his eyelids. This produces visions and leaves him blind for the rest of his life. Afterward they lead him to the room formed by the god's head. He remains there four years, dictating the futures of other men, as well as inventing their pasts.

Two nine-year-old girls bring him the flesh and milk of gazelles, and fowls basted with honey and figs. Eight times each day a dark-skinned youth comes bringing wood for the fire to light up the god's eyes, and incense to be burned. Every day the girls and the youth are different, but they have the same voices, the same lines in their palms, and their footsteps always sound the same.

One night when the four years are up, a drop rolls down his cheek, and while he is wondering what has become of his life and his past, they lead him to his final resting place.

THREE

The sensation of dizziness had not left him, and the road seemed to grow longer by the minute. They were waiting for him at the table when he arrived; his usual place there appeared to have been kept for him.

The theatre was empty save for them: three men and three women dressed as men. In the past their parents used to come to watch them, but now it was a long time since anyone had come.

At the usual hour the woman dressed as a priest opened the book upon which no one may cast his glance.

In earlier days they used to build a fire, around which they chanted their prayers. The best of these messages were answered. But it was a long time since they had made the fire. It was enough for them to tell each other their dreams and recount the stages in their progress.

The last time they met, the tallest of them declared that he no longer wished to possess a soul. The others were unable to convince him of its indestructibility. To reassure himself he put his hand into his pocket, and drawing a smile with his finger, felt the edges of the banknotes.

The woman was forty years old. The gold thread seemed to come from the cellar. She asked me to spread my legs. When the thread came out through my mouth I fought back the nausea. As if she were carrying something between her hands, she went down again into the cellar. I could sense the thread passing through me. Even though it became necessary to kill her, I had to know what she was hiding down there.

It was a blind room. The door was behind an old rug.

There are places where evil is converted into good. The men work the earth in another manner. The women love, and sit on the ground when they weave, and the fruit of their inventions is forbidden.

All the men would meet in the middle of the plaza, around a central pillar. The cords were beginning to be confused with skin and blood. When it was day once again the fire would have transformed him into a bird—a promise and a punishment.

(That night the only words that will be used in the songs will be those that recall the odor of the sea and distant sand.)

The final knot in the web is the fingernail of a black slave or god who has fought with a tiger.

He spent the night hidden in the belly of a young elephant. He had felled it by cutting the tendons with a long poniard. That afternoon he had covered himself with mud to conceal his odor. And with his ear flat against the ground he had waited for the herd to come down to the river to drink.

FOUR

I

I have forgotten what their houses were like outside. The interiors shone with every shade of blue, from pallid to deep. The silk was embroidered with diamonds arranged in the patterns of the stars in the sky.

The only animals to inhabit the place are felines (although I am certain I saw no cat). The people do not read, nor do they know of music or fire.

Their only sciences are magic and the cutting of precious stones. They do not believe in a god, but included in the few words they use there is invariably a certain particle whose meaning can only be translated as "the divine."

All I can remember, before I fell asleep, is that an old man was unweaving the silks of the house where I was staying, and that he left me alone in my room.

II

A legend tells of how the first man met God as he was walking along the road. To pass the time, he decided to regale the stranger with stories he had devised for his own pleasure on his solitary walks. In this way the concept of places and people came to God's mind.

Another legend, probably an older one, insists that the idea came, not from the first man, but from an angel who, tempted by the thought of seducing God, invented words and letters with which to write them, so that God, upon seeing them converted into stories, would then imagine a world of flesh. The angel was punished by being imprisoned in that world and that flesh.

III

All afternoon I had watched the little cloud. Now the sun was about to set and the wind was growing colder by the minute. Although it was changing in color, the cloud still had not moved. I got up. It seemed to be losing height; it grew smaller and heavier, until it was in front of my eyes. Through the vapor I could see a crystalline structure of absurd complexity. The sun had disappeared. I lay down again and fell asleep.

IV

To the north there is a damp black wall that rises in a curve to cover the sky. To the south the wall is broken by an iron-barred window. The light which comes in every twelve hours illumines the east and the west, where drawings and words cover the stones. The light is not from the sun. Air enters, filtered through guarded grillworks.

The path doubles back on itself several times before one reaches the summit. On the farther side of the mountain the forest is cut in half by a valley. A river flows there, and beside the river is a village. In all we are seventeen houses. We had divided the men into groups to patrol the valley. Within two hours after we gave the signal each man was at his post.

V

The taste she had in her mouth was mine. The taste that I had was one she could not know. It has in it something of her spine, of the back of her legs, and of the place where her legs separate. Her head, the jaw seen from between the two breasts. Her cheeks and her neck when it grows red, and her eyes when they are shut.

VI

It was my birthday and, as still happens to me, I felt uncomfortable. I had been born twelve years before.

My father gave me a thick, heavy book bound in brown leather. The impression of antiquity it made upon me was no less than my astonishment at finding that inside there was nothing but blank white pages, one after the other.

Beginning with that day each moment of happiness or despair, of desire or rancor, every new object, every face, was religiously recorded in the diary. Every day, sometimes every hour, each gesture . . .

VII

Many, many years ago they came to the village. They looked like three big birds, but they had arms and hands, and they used knives. In a coffer to which each one had a key, they kept the smallest and heaviest stone we had ever seen.

They lived among the people for six weeks, eating what we eat and sleeping in our houses. No one remembers seeing them lose their tempers or hearing them raise their voices. Three days before they left, they spoke to two young people, a man and a woman. When the sun rose, the five figures climbed up the path of rocks that loses itself on the side of the mountain.

They returned when night had come and gone three times. Then the strangers disappeared.

The young woman and her companion slept together for another three days. When they awoke, they told of how the oldest of the three had opened their foreheads with his finger while the other two reached into the coffer. Then, exactly at the moment when the sun ceased to be visible, they broke the tiny stone into two pieces, and the oldest fitted the pieces into the openings he had made in their foreheads.

No one seemed to understand or believe them. That day they left the village. Before it was lost to sight, he turned and saw the sad smoke hanging over the houses, and the tears came into his eyes. A black cloud covered the village and there was the barking of dogs.

SUNRISE

I

A man and his wife were listening to the night wind that comes up the hill from the sea. A moment ago there had been a clap of thunder, and she had said: "These pains are hell," and passed her hands over her belly. He had not answered. He was thinking of himself, and on the other side of his consciousness he imagined the shattered pieces of a crystal.

"I wish I were far away from here," she went on. Her inflection was clear; it held no doubt. "I know you have a lot of pain," he told her. He rose from the table and went to stand by the fire. The woman left the dining room, and he heard her go upstairs and shut a door. He leaned over to put more wood on the fire, thinking: Neither one of us is unhappy. To his right the curtains in front of the window moved, and the shadow of the wall that enclosed the garden stirred along its folds.

The heat of the flames was such that he moved away a few steps. As he approached the window he heard a moan. It seemed to come from outside. He pulled back the curtain to peer out. Above the trees a translucent cloud tempered the light of the half moon. He let go of the cloth and absently watched its movements. The moaning sound came again, and he felt his hands growing cold. He ran upstairs, opened a door, and his wife stifled a cry. "What's the matter?" she asked him. He noted a strange light in her eyes and detected a note of mockery in her voice. He shut the door and went back downstairs. "She's like a child," he thought. There was another moan; he decided it was the wind.

II

His hands were spread out above the embers. His stare was fixed and distant as innumerable images whirled through his mind—moments he had lived through with her: days he had forgotten, faces they had admired together, a sunrise and a lake, a scrap of pink paper and two small stones, and the boy who had assured them it was not a charm, afternoons and nights on a mountain. He took a few steps backward and sat down heavily in a chair facing the fire. As he sank down, there was a cracking sound, and he felt an intense pain in his spine. "I've broken in half," he said aloud; the hoarse sound of his voice frightened him. He remained sitting there. His leg muscles were languid. But at the same time he saw himself rise and pass in front of the fireplace into the hall and out of the house.

The half moon was sinking behind the path that leads down the hill and ends on the beach. He took a few more steps and stopped, looked around him and saw the shadow of the house; then he looked into the distance, at the long nebulous stripe between the sky and the sea. With a slight shudder which he himself provoked, he began to walk down the hill. Before he got to the beach he saw a flash of light on the water; there was a sound like raindrops falling, and then distant voices. He continued to walk. The slope became steeper, and without being aware of it, he began to run.

When he got to the beach he caught sight of a boat. Three men were rowing it, their backs to the sky; they were approaching the shore. They jumped into the water and beached the boat. They were naked. One of them covered himself with a blanket and set about gathering firewood. The other two, one behind the other, pulled in a long line attached to the stern of the boat. Black fish emerged, ten or twenty at each pull; the red of their gills shone in the moonlight. The fire grew and made shadows that flickered on the sand. He looked at the stars and thought: Perhaps they are holes, and their rays are ropes that other fishermen hold in their hands. It began to dawn; the men reached the end of the rope. He was cold, and he remembered the fire that had burned in his house. Later, he took his leave of the men and started back. The sand moved under his feet; he reached the path, and felt like running. "I won't go home," he thought. He rubbed his hand over his forehead and saw that he was sweating. His eyes looked softly at the sun as he ran up the hill.

THE MONASTERY

I

At the top, where the mountain meets the sky, there is a large building. It was once a monastery, but the monks abandoned it. One night Fray Angelo awoke uttering a scream. Other monks heard it: it was a long scream. When the others who slept on the lower floor found him, a stertorous whistling sound was still issuing from his throat. He was nearly naked. It looked as if several hands had ripped off his clothing, and his face was covered with deep scratches. The abbot ordered boiling water and cold water to be brought to the bed. Then the brother was tied to the bedposts. When morning came, Fray Angelo had died. The phenomenon recurred, with Fray Bartolo, with Fray Natalio, and with Fray Fortunato. Finally, admitting defeat, the abbot closed the monastery.

The building is empty now. It is a structure of three stories with a spacious cellar. In the center there is a courtyard where the brothers used to stroll as they prayed. On the ground floor are the chapel and the oratory, giving on the north; the kitchen and dining room face south; on the east there is a wall with only one door, and on the west the abbot's study with a small door leading into his assistant's room. On the two floors above there are thirty-six bedrooms, and in the cellar thirty-six tiny lightless cells.

II

The wind and the trees were making a kind of song. I remembered that when I had left the house my father had said: "When you come back, everything will be the same."

One gets to the monastery by a path that leads upward. As I walked, the branches on both sides scraped my shoulders and occasionally my cheeks. "They're bowing as I go by, to show that they recognize me," I thought to myself. "He's the son of the merchant," they would say when I could no longer hear them: "He wants to leave the world behind." Below, when I had turned around, I had seen the town out there, far away. I did not want to go back. In other times I used to walk to the edge of the island of houses and watch the sun go down behind the green (or red) countryside. It gave me a particular and inexplicable pleasure. But on later afternoons, although I kept walking and witnessed the coming of evening, nothing stirred inside me. I saw the light losing itself below the horizon; the twilights were like drops of water falling constantly to torture me. And at night the stars were useless points. What illness was causing this clouding of my thoughts? A slow darkness had come down over me, a cloud stretched across my horizon. But why? It was in the course of a dream that I discovered why: there was a sheet of paper on which, in letters that impressed me as being very ancient, was written: "The Cause of All Causes is God." Then the wind came and snatched the paper out of my hand, carrying it off.

Then I knew that the cause of my discontent was God. The sun was high in the sky when I awoke. While I waited for my parents—they would be returning from the warehouse—I looked on the map for the location of the monastery.

When I got to the end of the path my clothing was torn, and I could feel the scratches made on my face by the branches. I was at the top of the mountain. The wind whistled. I stepped across the threshold. The walls outside were covered with ivy; inside they were black. There was no roof, and the wind here made no sound.

It grew dark. I lay down on the floor and fell into a light, hesitant slumber halfway between sleep and wakefulness. What I saw was there, and at the same time seemed not to be. The walls altered and became white. In the center of the courtyard there was a fountain, and to the north of it, a tree. I stood up and went to sit under it. I saw the moon reflected in the water of the fountain. A shaft of light shot down out of the sky. "A spirit," I said to myself, almost awakening. Its garments were transparent, and underneath them there was a constant shifting and flowing of colors. But when I saw its face I was afraid, and with a silent cry I uttered the word "No." And it disappeared.

When I found myself alone, I began to have misgivings. A bit later a man came into the monastery. As he walked, his feet seemed not to be touching the floor. He came near and sat down in silence beside me. Then, "What are you looking for?" he asked me. His voice was low-pitched and mellow. "What are you looking for?" I repeated, to myself. The sound of the words spread in the silence. I was looking for rest, but the solitude and the silence bothered me. "Do you know Regina?" I asked, looking at him. He did not return my glance. "So, I can't help you," he told me. He stood up and went in the direction of the door. I ran after him and caught up with him. Then he stood still and stared at me. His face was smooth. "I don't know what I'm looking for; perhaps I don't know. . . ." I spoke with difficulty, staring at the floor, shaking my head. He went back to the fountain and I followed him. "Lie down and shut your eyes," I heard him say. I hesitated an instant, then did as he suggested. Even though I was aware that I was dreaming, everything was suffused with the essence of reality. His fingers touched my forehead. A painful spasm of cold passed through me. His other hand pressed on my throat. Two tepid drops hit my temple and then I heard them fall, one after the other, onto the floor. I heard: "Open! Open!" and I moved my eyelids: everything had changed. I was moving, losing consciousness, in the darkness. Behind me trailed a thread. Ahead, suspended in space, shone an object. It looked like an enormous coin. I remembered that I was dreaming.

I awoke. The sun was rising, and its rays came in through the doorway. A loud, insistent noise going on around me decided me to get up. I hurried to the door, and as I passed beneath the lintel I saw that it was swarming with tiny white insects. "Termites," I thought. After I had taken a few steps there was a dull sound behind me. I turned to look, and then ran all the way down to the town.

THE INHERITANCE

In that city there lived two women of humble circumstances, a mother and daughter, who were known to be witches. Whereas the mother was ordinary-looking and ugly, the beauty of the daughter, even though she was only fourteen years old, had been sufficient to cause a youth of lowly origins to kill himself.

The events related here took place when the daughter was already in her twenties. Her mother had died, leaving her in addition to a cottage, a skillfully drawn map. This document contained a series of designs which in one way or another represented the whims of several people, and which demonstrated how certain couples had been brought together in the way the old woman had devised.

One morning a woman sought out the daughter to tell her that she feared her husband was unfaithful to her. When the woman had told her story, they arranged another appointment at which it was understood that the girl would give her a remedy to calm her suspicions. But the woman did not return, and some weeks later when the girl heard of her death, she had an inkling of what had happened. It did not take her long to learn that the recently widowed man was very wealthy. Having made up her mind to punish him, she obtained a photograph of him and one of his son. She studied them carefully. The youth attracted her, and she decided that once the father was out of the way, she and the son could have a happy life together.

Then she began to watch carefully the actions of her intended victim without seeming to be spying on him. Finally, one afternoon she stood beside the highway waiting for his automobile to appear, a silver point on the horizon. When the man saw her waving by the roadside, he stopped the car. She leaned against it; he lowered the window and opened the door. As she had supposed, it was not difficult for her to get on familiar terms with him. When they arrived in the city she got out of the car not far from her house, and they said good-bye until the following day.

From the moment she had seen him she had felt revulsion toward him; thus it was easy for her to carry out her plan.

Not long afterward the two visited a house that belonged to him. It was in the mountains a few kilometers north of the city, and there she intended to strangle him with the ribbon that was wound around her head. They were rolling on one of the sofas upstairs and his eyes were shut in voluptuousness, when she unwound the ribbon and passed it around his neck. Her face expressionless, she pulled. The man's efforts to free himself came to nothing. When he was dead, she dressed him and left him lying there. She hurried out of the sitting room and on tiptoe crossed the hall that led to the bedroom. With deliberate violence she wrenched apart the glass case which enclosed the gold reliquary hanging on the wall above the bed, seized it and put it into her bag. When night came she buried it in the garden behind her house. Then she waited for two months to go by.

At the end of this time she began to frequent the café on the corner which the son of her victim used to visit on Saturdays. One fine day, as soon as she saw him sauntering along the sidewalk, she went out toward him and collided with him, giving him a push with her shoulder so that they both were thrown off balance. He apologized with embarrassment, and one glance was sufficient for her project to take a favorable turn.

They were married that same winter. But whereas he was happy, she began to fall prey to her conscience and to suffer from nightmares.One night she awoke with her hands at her throat. In spite of her husband's efforts to preserve her sanity, the subsequent sessions with a hypnotist and the ministrations of the doctors, in the space of two years she lost her reason. The cause of her madness was never established, but when she suspected, not without a certain glee, that she was going to die, she took her husband's arm and drew her free hand suggestively across her throat. He nodded calmly, to show her that he had already understood.

THE WIDOW OF DON JUAN MANUEL

It was eleven o'clock. A small wind blew through the house. His wife went to shut the window. He rolled his eyes, drew a deep breath, and expired.

She did not bewail his death.

At dawn one morning a week after his death, his ghost appeared. The face held no threat; at the same time, he was weeping. Don't be afraid, woman, he said. It's I. She became calmer and listened attentively. He had sat down at the foot of the bed and he told her: "A man spends his life hoping to rest finally, and when he dies he finds that he's just as he was at the beginning: ignorant. He's like someone who's taken drugs: he doesn't know where he is. Everything is made out of light. Without noticing how, he wakes up; the light is heavy, and he wishes he were blind."

As he talked, there was a knock at the door. Don Juan Manuel hastened to hide in the clothes closet. His wife covered herself and went to open the door. The wind and a shadow came in. There was no one. She shut the door, went back to the bedroom, and called to her husband. He was gone. She lay down on the bed, her eyes straying to the window which faced west. Thousands and thousands of drops were falling They formed a curtain, that consoled her as it darkened the landscape.

A strident sound brought her out of her revery. It had come from inside the house, from the direction of the dining room. She remained lying on the bed, never taking her eyes from the increasing rain. A taste of something wilted filled her mouth. She had no sooner heard the cry a second time when a face appeared at the window. It was Don Juan Manuel. He tossed in a flower which fell near the bed, scattering its petals, and then he faded from sight among the myriad raindrops. When it had stopped raining and was growing dark, she got up. The door giving from the bedroom onto the passageway was ajar. She peered through the crack: light was still coming in at the back of the house. Taking care to make no sound, she crossed the passageway. From where she was she could see the telephone. She reached it, dialed a number, and sat down on the dark wooden stool. "Reverend," she said, "please come." At the same moment, a blue and yellow bird that had been hiding in the lamp which hung above the dining room table, flew out of it and broke its neck against the windowpane.

THE SORCERER'S SON

In the shade of a tree near the center of the square a group of people had gathered. One man with a pale, greenish complexion seemed to be describing an involved fight. It was almost impossible to understand his words. His gestures were wide and violent; he touched his face, indicating his eyelids, bared his breast and a long scar that traversed his belly.

Later that night they explained that he was a sorcerer, and that what he had been relating that afternoon was the story of the birth of his son. He had told them that one morning when he stooped over to drink in the river, he had seen his face in the water. It was transformed: his eyes had been gouged out, and his lips were mixed up with his nose. He shook his head, and managed to see himself again as he really was. An aching had started up inside him. Walking with difficulty, at times even having to crawl, he moved upward along the path and came to a cave. He went in and sat down, breathless. On his abdomen he saw, or thought he saw, a fire burning. The flame leaned eastward, although there was no wind. He remained there in the dark for seven days, without eating, drinking or moving. One morning before dawn two tiny women the size of a head visited him. They danced, or struggled desperately, on top of his abdomen.At the end, one of them lay dead, near his groin. The other slashed open his belly with a stone blade and hid inside the wound, carrying the body of the other with her. When the sorcerer thought he was already dead, a bird like a ray of light flew out of his belly. It described a white circle and then a red one, above his body, and disappeared into the distant sky.

A WIDESPREAD BELIEF

I

It is a widespread belief that greatly successful men do not have clear consciences. An Italian who came on Sundays to the Café Roma used to expound this idea. He would pause, shut his eyes, and summarize: "They have dealings with the Devil, or somebody like him." His listeners would agree.

After drinking a bottle of red wine all by himself, Don Alessandro—this was his name—would make his confession. His father had been a man of great wealth. He would take out a billfold and extract from it the photograph of his father. "He was very proud," he would say, and his voice held a note of recrimination.

In his youth his father had been in North Africa. There, in a café called Al Hafa, Hassan spied him for the first time, and followed him through the market all afternoon. Finally the Moslem touched him on the shoulder. He turned. The Moslem smiled and spoke to him in his tongue. They became friends.

II

Once when Don Alessandro, the son, had finished his tale, I accompanied him to his house. He had told of how the two young men had formed a business. Both of them traveled here and there for many years. They grew old and rich. Then their sons, Don Alessandro and Aziz ben Hassan went on with the business. They owned a small fleet of boats which plied between Tangier and Gibraltar. One afternoon during a storm three of the boats disappeared, and with them Aziz. Don Alessandro searched for his partner. Years later he saw him in the south of France, drinking tea at a sidewalk café. Don Alessandro paid four thousand francs to a youth, and Aziz died with his throat cut.

Don Alessandro walked slowly: it was the wine. I had to help him up the stairs. "They're interminable," he told me. Afterward I put him to bed. He was pale; he repressed a sigh. Feebly I said the words: "Aziz was my father." His gaze wandered to the window. Three small birds were perched on the wire fencing outside. He would have run downstairs and pushed open the door, but he was too old. He only wet himself lying there on the bed. I remembered the last photograph of my father, on the sidewalk with blood in his mouth.

I had a knife in my hand, and I looked at the old man. His skin gleamed like metal, his eyes shone. "I'm tired," he said.

For fourteen years I had dreamed of cutting his throat.

I went out of the room. The door slammed shut.

III

Slowly I went down the stairs. Before I got to the front door I turned and mounted the steps again. My hand fell softly on his bed. He closed his eyes. "Thank you," he said, because he would live a few years longer. I stood up, hid the knife under my shirt, and left him.

The most trustworthy men maintain that God's right arm will deal the blow which will settle all debts. But only He, Allah, knows everything.

I hurried away.

THE RIVER BED

I

When he pulled back the curtains, the light blinded him for a moment. He recognized the valley and the distant grey mountains; the flavor of his dreams, which he had learned to retain, faded in his mouth. A row of palms cuts the valley in half, hiding the river bed; from there the voices of the invisible children reached him as they collected rocks with which to build their walls and towers. Presently he raised his eyes to stare at the sky, and after thinking: "Each day that goes by it looks farther away," he turned, dragged his feet across the rug, and fell back into bed. He stretched out his arm and touched one of the books that lay there covered with dust. He opened it. Before he had finished reading the first sentence, he let it fall to the floor.

II

He had never felt utter sadness until now. When the sun had gone down, he went out of the house and listened to his own voice saying: "My God!" Often he had known silence, but this evening for the first time he wished its enchantment could last forever, around him, over the valley, and if possible, above the sky. He walked, and soon he came to the highest tower the children had built. He kept his eyes fixed on the sand, and he could feel the heat given off by his body.

When he realized that a woman was observing him from the other bank of the dry river bed, he regretted that there was no water flowing, since he wanted to be alone. Her smile was forthright. Salt and sand crackled under her feet; she came up to him and stood beside him. Then she bent over and picked up a round stone. She held it out to him, and he took it. He spread his cape on the ground and they sat down. At that moment there came the distant sound of a voice (it was the name of God) and he stood up. He fastened the cape around his neck and ran back to the village. Before he went under the archway of dried mud, he dropped the stone he held in his hand, and heard it hit the ground. In the street, as he turned a corner, he saw something shining from the wall. In between the bricks was a white brooch. He pulled it out and fastened his cape with it. When he got home, his mother said: "That brooch. Where did you find it?" "A woman gave it to me," he told her. "We met today in the market." He sat down at the table and began to eat.

III

When he had finished eating, he shut himself in his room. He went to the window and remembered that recently the white of his eyes had begun to show below the pupils. "I'm not well," he thought. "Why?" He would have liked to pray, but he could not. Nevertheless, he joined his hands and touched his forehead with his fingers. The wind was blowing hard, and he imagined that the earth had started to revolve more quickly. "Tomorrow is the first day of winter," he recalled. "At night there will be music."

When he awoke in the morning he had his hands between his thighs. He got up and looked in the mirror. He saw his black shoulder-length hair and reached out to touch the glass with his fingernails. Then he went out into the garden, and the cold air filled his lungs. The trees laden with fruit, the colorless sky, and on the path his shadow swaying in front of him, all served to increase his melancholy. "I wish I weren't here," he thought, imagining an impossible place where the wind never blew and the soul did not exist. He had walked so far on the sand that his legs had tired. He lay down beside the dry trunk of a tree, and touched the rough grey surface with his hands. A dark translucent resin oozed out of the wood. With some difficulty he shifted his position and brought his lips into contact with the substance. His muscles relaxed. "If only my life were different," he thought. "Even though I'm here, I'm not here."

IV

Behind him, he heard someone say his name. He opened his eyes, turned his head slowly, and saw the woman who had given him the stone. He still felt a great weariness, and within himself a sensation of cold like that which comes after weeping. She made a friendly gesture; he looked away. His cheek rubbed the bark of the tree and his face broke into a smile. He stood up and began to walk away, hastening his step. A continuous, low-pitched sound was in his throat. "If I wanted," he said to himself. "But no. I don't want to." He began to run. Soon he stopped, and felt the pounding of blood in his head. The woman, who had followed him, now stopped beside him. "What's the matter?" she asked him. He did not reply. He looked at her eyes and silently repeated: "*I'm here but I'm not here.*" He was about to say something, but then, as one, they glanced around them: there was no one in sight. She bent down and drew a circle in the sand, and with a finger she marked a point in its center. With difficulty, he said: "Good." They started to walk, side by side, following the bed of the river, and they did not stop when it grew dark. "They'll think we're dead," she remarked. "In the town?" he said. "It doesn't matter. We won't go back."

Somewhat later they came to an enormous boulder; the river bed continued on each side of it. Then, very faintly, from some village in the region, came the call: God is the most powerful. He knelt down and took a little sand in his hands. She lay beside him and pulled off the cloth that had hidden her hair. Moving closer to her, he said: "It has rained in the mountains. Tonight there may be water in the river." Then like water meeting with water, the two became one.

SON AND FATHER

I

A man dallied for two hours on his way home, where his wife was waiting for him. He lay down beside her and managed to get to sleep a little before daybreak. All night he had been listening to her as she ground her teeth in her sleep. It had seemed to him that both he and she were wrapped in a dark cloth; he covered his eyes with his left arm. He recalled the books he had read that afternoon; he recalled the library. He pondered. Words fluttered in his mind like insects around the steady light of a hot lamp: the Father, the Son, being, non-being, the presence and the spirit. It seemed to him that his God and we in the world were incongruous, and that we were all one. He thought of daily life, and saw that he was making it into a nightmare — perhaps an eternal one. He hoped to clarify his thoughts, but unexpectedly he found himself imagining the face of some director of magic, high above one of the great cities. He understood that it would be impossible to find him. It seemed self-indulgent of him to have gone into the city, which he considered to be the chessboard where an unfair game was played. He thought of life, or of his desire to live, as the result of long-range plans and operations prudently foreseen by such a demigod — or such demigods — with dubious intentions.

He needed air; he longed to leave everything behind, and fell asleep.

His wife awoke. It was his habit to discuss his thoughts with her. With the help of the daylight she would endeavor to vary the course of his reflections.

II

But, the same day, the man went to the town where his father lived. He found him asleep during his siesta hour. In order not to wake him, he went outside and walked about, admiring the growth of the plants and flowers in the garden. He breathed freely.

He saw his father later, and the two took a walk to a clearing on the side hill. The sun was turning red. He looked at his father and smiled. He turned to stare at the clouds in the west—the sun had now disappeared—and thought: "He doesn't know what the infinite is." The light grew dim and each became invisible to the other. On the way back they both stumbled several times.

After dinner they went to bed.

The old man coughed. A bit later the son also coughed; he was disturbed. Little by little he was becoming more like his father. When he laughed, although he tried to prevent it his laugh was that of the other. "Suppose he died," he thought.

The old man coughed again and opened his eyes, without being fully awake. It seemed to him that his son's breating was growing fainter. He saw an enormous fly come buzzing through the window and land on his pillow. Then he awoke: he was alone in the room.

The son was in the garden. His conscience was bothering him, and he stared at the slight mist that rose from the lawn.

The old man sat on his bed and leaned over to reach his clothing. He stood up and began to dress; he had to lean against the wall. Near the foot of the bed he noticed a bent pin; he left it there. "Son!" he called as he went out of the house.

During breakfast the father patted his son on the shoulder as he thought: "We're just alike."

THE LOST KEY

Was no one expecting him? He rang again at the blue door. Nothing. Yet, on the floor above, one of the windows was open. He had forgotten to shut it. He felt for the key in the bag he wore over his shoulder, and did not find it. He realized that he had lost it, and set out down the cobbled alley. He ran. It was already evening.

He wiped the sweat from his forehead. Using both hands, he searched for the key underneath the tables and chairs of a tavern. Aware of his posture, he began to smile at himself, but then his face froze again with dread. He went out into the street and looked again in his bag. The key was not there. Moreover, he had no money on him; he carried some loose papers, a notebook, a box of matches and a pen. The key had disappeared.

As he made his way back in the direction of the blue door, he experienced a sensation which was new to him. He listened to his own heartbeats: they were everywhere. His hands were in his pockets, pushing against his thighs. He stopped in front of the door, and with both hands out flat, gave it a push. There was a squeak and the door opened. Instead of going in, he stepped back. He thought of the woman who took care of his birds, and then he thought of the back courtyard, of the wall that surrounded it, and the iron spikes against the sky. Someone might have got over it. It was not an impossibility that there was someone inside. At that moment the person could be watching him from upstairs, through the bathroom window. He did not dare look up. It occurred to him to walk away, but he went in. There was no light in the entrance hall. He stepped ahead with his arms extended in front of him, feeling his way, until he located the candelabrum. He felt in his bag for the little box of matches, struck one, and lighted the candles. With three of them burning, he took the candelabrum to light his way up the stairs. He began to climb, looking upward, his hand on the banister. The ceiling seemed to be swirling above his head. He made a misstep and lost his balance. He tried to step backwards, but his foot got entangled in the cuff of his trousers. He shut his eyes before he landed on the lower steps. Then he heard the cracking of his ribs, and he stopped breathing for a moment. When he opened his eyes, he saw that the candles had rolled beyond his reach. One of them was still burning. There was a bitter taste in his mouth. He got up and seized the candle. As he lifted it, the flame went out. The darkness that followed blinded him. He stepped a bit along the floor and ran into the candelabrum. He crouched down, keeping his breathing silent. Finally, he lifted his arm in search of the wall. Dragging himself along, he brushed the wall with his breath, until he found the bottom step. He began to climb again. The sweat on his hands stayed on the banister. He was losing the sense of distance; his extremities seemed to be growing longer, and he felt himself in the midst of nothingness. In the darkness he imagined a world whose meaning could not be grasped, but which at the same time was real. A gust of wind touched his face, and the slamming of the front door in the draft dispersed his thoughts. He shook his head in a manner that was scarcely human. His eyes roved in the utter darkness; fear created irrational forms that moved around him. Only the edge of the stair against his thigh remained fixed. All the rest could as easily not have been there. Two distinct knocks came from the entrance hall; someone was at the door. As he stood up there was a peculiar sound. It was the bolt sliding, and the door hit the wall as it opened. He could not bring himself to speak. He moved to the right and his foot touched the bag. He bent over; from where he was, he could not see who had opened the door, but he could discern the outline of his clothing. The faint light coming in from the street made that much visible. He went back down the steps he had mounted and, with his arms in front of him, rushed toward the front door to throw himself upon the figure. But the figure which had entered moved swiftly in its grey cloak, and managed to elude him.

The second man seemed to know the house better than the first; he ignored the darkness. He ran up the stairs two steps at a time, and after walking slowly around the upper story, started back down, lighting his way with a torch which he held over his head. He took a step down and stopped to listen. He took another step, and another. As he went down, his expression grew somber: he failed to understand what he saw. What could be the meaning of the countless masks hung on the wall, and the dissected animals? It disturbed him. The trunk of the tree that grew in the inner patio had been painted red, and in the branches there were several birds pretending to be alive. The sound of a footstep within the house made him turn his head, but he could see nothing. He fitted the torch into a black iron staple, and went to pick up the candelabrum. Then he noticed the bag lying on the floor. He put in his hand and found the pen and the papers. The notebook was missing. He hesitated for a moment and, before running toward the street, went to put out the torch. Just as he had extinguished the flame, he heard someone approaching him on tiptoe from behind. He jumped and wheeled around, but now it was dark and little was visible. He became aware of a shadow, not far from him, under the arcade. He rushed at it. He was mistaken, but he was certain that there was someone else in the house. It would be hard to say what he felt. He was confused by the quiet. Wrapped in himself, he was lost in his slightly trembling body. There was a damp tingling on the back of his legs. Having no idea of what else to do, he hid himself behind a large urn. He remained there for a minute or so. He was beginning to grow used to the darkness, and he felt around for something with which to defend himself. His hand found a loose tile; he pulled it out and brandished it in the air, conscious both of the absurdity of the gesture and of the fear mounting inside him. He felt like jumping up and attacking, but attacking what? A dog barked outside the house. He counted to ten barks, and slowly got up. He intended to cross the entrance hall and go out. There was light in the street. He had not taken four steps when there was a whipping sound at his back, and a machete chopped into his shoulder. He fell face down, and as he fell his head made a noise (scarcely audible outside itself) which lashed from side to side in his entrails. He no longer distinguished between the cold floor and his own cheek, and he stared obliquely at a prolonged greenish glow; it seemed to him like a fissure in the lengthy darkness. He reached for it with his hand, and the thread of light flashed, clipping at his face. Thoughtlessly he raised his hand to the wound. He shut his eyes to the shadows that writhed around him. The apex of his consciousness (to give it a name) spun on its imaginary axis, hastening toward its center. As if it were from very far away he heard the irregular and repeated barking of the dog. He listened to the footsteps of the other man as he went away, and they sounded huge. The weapon fell heavily to the floor. There was a pause, then a noise. He understood that the door had been shut.

The first man was running down the street. He had the notebook with him, pressed between his belt and his sweaty belly. For half an hour he ran on; his flanks moved with his rapid breathing. Following a straight path, he was coming near to a lone tree which stood out in silhouette at the top of a desolate hill. He had opened the notebook as he hurried along, and with his eyelids scarcely open, he was reading. When he was under the tree in its shelter, he stood still and looked in all directions: there was no one in sight. He examined the branches that stood out against the night sky, went around the trunk, and having made sure that he was alone, stooped and pounded three times with his fist on a board which lay hidden in the dust. Carefully he removed the board and, leaning on it with one hand, let himself down as far as his waist into the orifice beneath. He let the notebook fall, and continued to look downward as it disappeared from sight, vertical in its silent descent. Climbing out of the hole, he covered over the emptiness with the board. Then he stretched out supine on the ground. He was satisfied. The names and the verdicts he had read (it is not permitted to mention them) would remain a secret. He would have liked to fall asleep, but it was not possible.

THE BEGGAR'S KNIFE

The dream that he had had earlier, before disembarking in the city where his parents lived, was repeated, this time without coming to its end. They are in the water, he and five tall clumsy men who surround him. Several fingernails come in contact with his skin: he feels no pain, only disgust. In order to keep his head above the water he is obliged to kick, and his legs graze their legs. He is very tired. He takes a deep breath and lets himself sink. An indefinite length of time goes by before he realizes that he can breathe in the water. His lungs swell; there is a sensation of well-being. He is lying on a bed of sand, and he looks up at the surface where the legs of the others are churning the water.

A gust of cold wind awoke him. A cylindrical lamp swung above his head and the shadows made the room lengthen and shrink. It took him a few seconds to understand where he was. The air smelled of rain. He said to himself in a low voice without conviction: "It's all right. I'm in the hotel." He remained awake until dawn. At noon he dressed, wet his face, and went down the twisting stairway with seven turnings and out into the street. It struck him that he was holding his body in an uncomfortable position. He tried to straighten up, but was stopped by the sharp

CONTENTS

o

quired: "Everything all right?" He said it was, and leaned his head back. Someone asked for music; there was the sound of whining voices as five beggars entered and fanned out among the smokers.

He glanced down at himself: the outlines of his hands and thighs were indistinct. Half asleep, he recalled a thought that once had occurred to him, and which he considered prophetic: "At the moment of my death I shall know who I am." He shut his eyes, or they shut of their own accord. Four or five men, their hands interlocked, were turning in a slow circle. He noted that these men were in the room with him. With irony he said to himself: "Since I want to die, I shan't die." Still toying with this idea, he was stopped by the hand of one of the beggars. "Help me," said the man's eyes. Knowing his pockets were empty, he pretended to search for a coin.

The beggar touches him on the hand, this time with greater boldness. He says no and simulates a smile. Out of the corner of his eye, he thinks he sees someone signaling to him, and turns to look. The beggar seizes his trouser-leg, and he pushes him away with a gesture of repugnance. The dirty face suddenly alters, takes on the color of violence. The man recoils, swiftly flashes a knife, and throws himself upon him. He feels something cold in his throat, his mouth fills with blood, his vision blurs. He feels hands pushing into his pockets, and he hears voices which he does not understand.

Two men carried him to the beach and left him on the sand. It was then that he knew where the wound was: it went across his neck from one side to the other. He doubted that the river was close at hand. He could not hear it. Like a man attempting to wake himself up, he shook his head, and realized that the cut was real. His eyelids came together and he was startled by a certitude. "I know that beggar. Who is he?" With his eyes still shut, because he could not open them, he crawled in the direction of the river.

He awoke exhausted, with the taste of chloroform in his mouth. That morning he crossed over countless times from wakefulness into sleep. In the afternoon two doctors came, and he understood that he was not dead. It was foggy outside. The next day the wind blew and the sky cleared in the west. He had dreams, but he could not recall anything but a black beach. Ten identical days went by, all of them interminable. The morning of the eleventh day he felt better. It would be possible to continue his trip southward down the river. Toward evening the sky covered over and it rained.

The next day he called his father, who answered the telephone himself. At first the conversation was chilly. When the son explained where he was calling from, the tone of the other voice altered; it assured him he would come and see him. He swallowed three pills and slept until noon of the following day, when he was awakened by the footsteps and the voice of his father. They talked together in leisurely fashion for a long time, settling their affairs. They had lunch together at the hotel, and in the afternoon they took a car to the docks on the river and hugged one another.

There was a muttering of voices on the pier. The son started up the gangplank, the ropes swayed slightly. The deck was crowded. He had a sense of foreboding. A few vendors were shouting their wares for the last time. He saw that he was the last passenger to have boarded the boat. Two seamen were about to unhook the gangplank; the vendors ran by, jostling him, and rushed down to the pier. He looked down there: his father was facing in the other direction. He felt a cold stab of fear: he had seen the beggar standing a few steps away. He wanted to shout or move, but because of the wound his voice failed him, and his legs would not obey. Calmly, with a silent laugh, he thought: "It can't be." A dagger tore into his throat. His waist struck against the railing. Slowly he thought: "I'm not going to die." His feet rose from the deck, his head was suddenly beside his knees, the sky whirled around. As he is falling he tells himself that he has died before, that he has been a mineral, a tree, an animal, a man, that he will cease to exist. He heard the splashing of water. A few concentric ripples formed around him. There was the hiss of foam, and the people on the pier stared down at the water.

REPORTS FROM CAHABON

I

It was one of the months in the rainy season — the first, second or third. A sanctuary had recently been constructed in the wilderness. Hidden by the dark and fog a man came there. Far away in a village the old men without beards were drinking. With half-shut eyes (the liquor) they were remembering: a small cross and the candlesticks, the boar's fast blood as it was cut into pieces, its heart buried beneath the round pool at the center of the temple, the four piles of flesh in the four corners, midnight, the mist, and the head (of the boar) opposite the hermitage.

"So that the walls won't fall down," the old people used to say.

"To get rid of bad luck." "So nothing will happen."

—From an informant of Cahabón. Found by Rafael Cabarrús S.J.

II

A man was looking for us. He wanted to learn about our customs. He came to see us at the house.

It is dangerous to speak of *custom*; possibly he did not understand what we told him.

We took him to the mountain and showed him the little cross and the candlesticks, and the neck of a dead rooster. The man seemed to understand, but he was not afraid, and this did not please the god.

We came back to the house and drank and ate.

In the morning the man fell sick, and he remained lying on a mat. I went to the mountain, asked permission, and pulled up some roots from the edge of the stream. I was thinking of my wife. I went to sell the roots and waited for it to get dark. Then it began to rain. I went back to my house and looked in through the window. The two of them were there, naked, sitting on the mat. I felt heavy, as if I couldn't breathe: it was the *mu* touching me. The man stood up and said to my wife: "I've got to piss. I'm going outside." "Do it here," she said. "There's a knothole there in the wall." The man put his sex into the hole and began to urinate. Then I saw the hand of the *mu* grab the organ and cut it off with a red machete. The man fell and died urinating. The *mu* gave me his sex and told me to grill it and give it to my wife to eat.

I have it here, in my game-bag. I'm going to give it to her. If she eats it, it will make her very thirsty. she'll go to the river to drink, and she'll swallow so much water that her stomach will burst.

—From El Viajero, *by Moises Bá.*

III

The white man's cornfields are frightening places. A tall, gleaming black man strides through them.

A voyager went alone through the night. His eyes were nearly shut with fatigue, and so he lay down in the shelter of a rock. "Rock is the flesh of God, who is in the sky," he said to himself gravely. Soon he fell asleep. But the rock spoke to him. "Come into me, because someone means to do you harm." And the man incorporated himself into the rock.

When the tall gleaming black man appeared, he took the body of the other in his arms; he crushed it, raped it and stuffed it into a leather sack. He went on his way, and when morning came he opened the sack, and saw that he was carrying a pile of pebbles.

—From an informant of Las Verapaces.

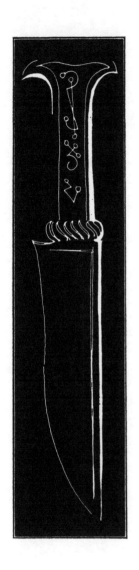

THE HEART OF GOD

I

God is something very small. It is the smallest thing that can exist in any world. Something very tiny and vague which, more than any other thing, likes to change its abode.

Sometimes it hides behind a book, or in the sound of a voice. In the eyes of a tiger or under the wings of a falcon. In a stone, just as in a cloud. In the hair of a woman or in the arrow shot by a hunter with perfect aim.

II

My legs were still trembling when I arrived at the house. It would be impossible to say what had happened. I have no idea of how long we fought. With difficulty I reached the bathroom. Without looking into the mirror I began to wash off the blood that covered my face.

III

God's heart has undergone a change, as have its faces.

Before men existed, god was like the animals, which later became sacred. And even longer ago, it was like the trees or like water.

THE BOOK

The book founders when it goes needlessly into the relation of certain pleasures.

Before the start of the voyage, it tells of a bathroom. It describes the hot water issuing from the tap, and it pauses to recall the sound it made. It speaks of the light coming in through the window and of soapsuds and of the memories that return as he bathes.

Afterward, or even during the bath, someone knocks at the door. He is handed a letter which he reads quickly. He dresses and eats something, packs a valise and takes some money from a box. Then he goes to see the friend who sent him the letter.

They talk a while, he spends the night there, and early the following morning he leaves from a port.

Days later he arrives in a city he calls Ogman. He decides to stop over there, in order to summon up memories of the sound an anchor makes as it drops into the water, and the sound made by the chains that attach a ship to the dock.

The port looks like a market. Without his being aware of it, a boy, or a youth with the face of a boy, dark-skinned, is waiting for him. He calls him by name. Then he leads him far down a narrow alley, until they reach a blue door in a white wall. Surely he is afraid. He mentions many dark eyes and strange smells. They have walked for two hours before arriving at the door, and the author busies himself noting down what he sees: rare plants, dissected snakes, dried roses, and the recently severed heads of goats or sheep, women with everything covered save their eyes, incenses of various hues, and swords and daggers adorned with skins and precious stones. They stop and his guide gives four raps on the door.

There is something different and unexpected in that house. Music sounds continuously. As one listens to it, one becomes confused. The old man who opened the door asks him to sit down at the table, scarcely distinguishable from the floor. Presently he brings a bottle of something dark, along with two identical stone mugs. He fills them and swallows the contents of one, gesturing to the other man to do likewise.

Although at first he was pleased by the interior lighting, it now begins to bother him. When he looks at his host, it seems to him that the man's gaze pierces his skin.

Still neither one of them speaks. Suddenly he feels the need of viewing himself in a mirror; he glances around the room, but sees none.

The old man gets up and goes into the adjoining room. The house has no doors between the rooms — only weighted curtains.

The music is dying away. The light grows feeble: one can sense the arrival of night. From behind the curtain in the next room a voice begins to intone. The rhythm and some of the melody he recognizes, but he is unable to make out the words. He stands up and the voice grows clearer. The curtain moves slightly, as if stirred by the wind. Then it seems to him that he is looking at a girl, and he confuses her silhouette with the shadow of the old man. He takes a step forward, his vision clouds, and the shadow and the silhouette disappear. At that point the book ends.

THE RAIN AND OTHER CHILDREN

I

The sun had not yet finished rising. There was only the sound made by the earth as it turns, interrupted, perhaps, by the flight of a bird or the sliding of a snake.

I was coming from my house. At my side I carried a sack of seeds, and in a little bag tied around my neck I had feathers whose colors changed as one moved them.

When I got to the village I saw them going by in the direction of the temple. All four were wearing dark brown robes. The first time I had seen them I had been only a child, and already I despised them. I waited and let them pass by without seeing me.

I crossed the market square, went into the little house at the end of the row, and sat down on the floor to wait. I set the seeds on a white cloth and the feathers on a red one. I looked at them absently when they came in. I gave them the things and went back to my house.

In the night I fell asleep talking with the god, and I reminded him that I had done what I was supposed to do. I asked him for rain and corn.

II

Four naked men came into my mother's house. She looked at me with dread, as someone who sees a thing he has seen many times. One of them seized me by the hair. She was crying, but they did not touch her.

They tied my hands with a black rope. The five of us went off down the road, which seemed to go on forever between the trees. They spoke to me to set my mind at rest, but I could not listen to them. There was a sound enveloping me, an infinite noise, like the sound of a jaguar's footsteps. The water they gave me to drink had a sweet aftertaste. We came to one of the neighboring villages, stopped, and went into a very old house. Inside was a man who freed my hands; the others left me alone with him. He told me to follow him, and we walked until we came to a temple built of tall, carefully cut stones. We started to climb slowly. As we went up, the man talked to himself. But he was speaking with reference to me; he spoke of my past life as though he had known me. He described my future, and he talked of the rain and of other children.

III

People were blaming me. They said that I was responsible for the drought. That I held the rain in my hands, that I could make it come, and that no one else could.

I thought of running away, because I did not want to perform the sacrifice, but they watched me constantly. I was forced to make up my mind and tell myself that there was no way of avoiding it. Once I had done what I must, rain would fall.

So I climbed up to the peak of the temple where I stood between two men. They laid the boy on a coverlet of white petals. My hand struck with force. The black edge of the stone slashed the skin, and blood stained the white petals. I took his heart, still beating, and placed it inside the mouth of the stone face. Then I kicked the small body, which rolled down the steps until it hit the ground.

A YELLOW CAT

Before falling asleep he twisted for two hours between the sheets; thus the nightmare may have been a result of what he had eaten earlier that night. When he awoke he laid his hands over his swollen stomach. Slowly he got up, thinking of the bathroom. Once he was there, washing his face, he began to remember.

He was in a carriage drawn by four horses, passing by a cafe in a street he did not recognize. The horses stopped two blocks farther on. He got out and began to walk. At that moment it was no longer the same street. It was wide and full of people and theatres.

He entered a house where he was received by two two men covered with black wool. Saying nothing, they led him to the rear door. Outside, a rowboat was waiting; it was to take them to the ship at the other end of the garden. His dead grandfather was aboard, expecting him. When they saw one another they embraced warmly. They kissed, looked into each other's eyes, and smiled. Just then a priest came in. He cast a reproachful glance at the old man, who had a bottle in his hand. The latter made a gesture of excusing himself, and they both disappeared from view for a discussion which took place behind a grill.

He went to the room where he slept. There was a yellow cat on his pillow. When he took off his clothes to rest for a while, the cat sprang at him and dug its claws into him. Pain rose into his throat like shattered glass, then sank to his stomach. He lay down in bed and was able to see the sky and its stars through the tiles of the roof.

NINE OCCASIONS

I

Although she will not be able to remember it, the concept of emptiness came to her when she was just beginning to talk. At nightfall her mother had left her alone in her room. She got out of the crib; she moved this way and that, taking short steps, and stopped in front of the window. Never before had she contemplated the night; her gaze wandered through the space between certain stars and others, without following any determined course. Her head spun and her breathing became a mere whisper.

II

He was sitting with his back against the break-water, letting the sand run between his fingers. He had been strolling aimlessly, and had come out at the beach, where he took off his shoes and walked south-ward.

He looked at his feet as he went along; several times he had raised his head and noticed the darkness that surrounded him. Once he had stood still, because far away on the sea a light was flashing. It was then that he thought: "Go back home," but he continued to walk. He had the feeling that he was about to discover something.

After crossing the bridge over the river, he found the breakwater. He touched the rock, to be certain, and sat down to rest.

III

The wind blowing over the wall and the beating of a bird's wings were the only sounds he could hear.

One of the little streets makes a curve and descends toward the west. It is a narrow street, seldom used. It goes by the houses of the poor, afterwards becoming a path which cuts through the woods and comes to an end where there is a wall. An old man lives there in a cave. The night when he left the world behind (he had already given away his worldly goods in order to attain merit in heaven) a woman recognized him and asked him for alms. In the folds of his clothing he had hidden the idol to which he prayed. He took it out and gave it to the beggar woman.

(Not many believe it, but whoever dreams of a black animal with smooth skin and the voice of a woman has met with an angel. He can climb upon its back and return to his place of origin, or he can turn from it, saying: "You're nothing more than a dream," and then die.)

IV

One afternoon a little before twilight a woman was watching rain as it dripped from the eaves of a house into a puddle that was turning pink with the clouds. She saw it as it began to leave the drainpipe, and she studied the circles made by the drops on the surface of the puddle. When the water was completely dark, she went toward the city.

Upon arriving at the library, she found it already shut. She smashed the glass of one of the doors and went in. As she moved this way and that, she stared with an anguished expression at the books on their shelves. She opened one of them, laid it on a table and leaned over it. Lighting a piece of paper, she applied it to the pages of the book. When it was flaming, she put it back with the others.

It began to rain when she went out into the street. The first book had burned, and those around it were smoldering. She went home; the streets were deserted.

Her father was seated in front of the oven. The noise of the knocker against the door roused him from his sleep. He crossed the entrance hall and asked: "Who is it?"

"I," was the answer. "It's I." And he opened the door.

V

He was in the dark, bent over a small wooden table. A struggle within him was reaching its climax. He looked around. There was not enough light to see them, but he guessed the walls of the room. For several hours he had been here, pulling at the threads of memory.

On the little table were a glass of water, a notebook (his diary) and a penknife. He lifted the knife to
examine the blade, cut off the top button of his shirt,
and undressed. He ran the sharp point of the blade
along his thighs, and drew a circle and a spiral on his
belly. With the knife raised to eye-level, a ray of light
from a crevice in the window flashed in his fist. Then
he let his arm fall back onto the table. He looked at
the wooden surface; it seemed to him that he was con-
versing with his hand, with the diary, with the yawn-
ing abyss. He rose and opened the window. The room
was flooded with the white light of the moon. Taking
up the notebook, he ripped out its pages.

VI

The preceding afternoon had been very hot; two
men dressed in grey had been cursing; the shopkeep-
ers had gone down to the square and there were
fights. When night came there was an orgy.

At the entrance to one of the small inns, a group
of beggars counted their coins by the light of a feeble
lamp; they insulted each other and lay down with
their cheeks against the ground.

A man with grey hair was staying in one of the
rooms at the back of the inn; he listened to the voices
that came from the garden and looked vaguely at the
glass in the window.

At ten o'clock he stopped reading and lay down
on the miserable bed. A fine dust covered the walls of
the room; he felt an unpleasant sensation on his

palate. He was alone and he felt as though he were bound by a chain. He crossed his arms over his abdomen. Inside him a low voice kept repeating: "You will always be alone, because you want to be alone, because you deserve to be alone." It was essential to change that. He got up and turned off the light. Then he lay down again and shut his eyes. The darkness agreed with him. He felt the breath that came out of his nostrils touch his lips, his abdomen, even his hands. The voice inside that had tormented him had slowly faded. Darkness had been followed by silence, and silence by calm. When he heard himself say: "The chain is breaking," he fell asleep.

VII

The tension caused by the silence had become unbearable.

They were sitting beside the road, and he glanced at her out of the corner of his eye as they built the fire. They had known each other for many years; it seemed to him that she did not suspect his recent interest in her; it had come suddenly, unforeseen.

She recalled the second night she had seen him; (at that moment he was touching his forehead). She had dreamed that one of her eyelashes had fallen into his wine. He had not noticed it, and had swallowed it. And later, when the breeze came up off the sea, she had lighted a taper and had knelt, thinking of him.

VIII

What tormented her was uncertainty. Because she never knew whether what she was doing was the right thing or not. Her conscience did not seem to her a trustworthy instrument; many times she had been wrong. She doubted herself; she doubted everything. She wanted to rest, but she went to look at herself in the glass. She did not understand her eyes, her lips, or her pointed nose.

At daybreak she lay on her bed with her eyes open. She began to blink, without knowing why. Each time she opened and shut her eyes, the present moment grew richer. The circle went on widening; she felt a slight dizziness. It was her pupils contracting.

VIX

"The road that goes down the hill" she would tell me, "stops before it gets to the lowest part. And the harder you try to find a path, the more it all changes."

I remember her white figure framed by the door. And I remember, in the background, the sandy plain in the sunlight, and the sound of the river. I would hear her thoughts, and as they moved ahead it seemed to me that I was getting to know her better. At the same time I realized how strange she was. "Who am I?" she would ask aloud. She was assailed by doubts, and it was impossible to guess what was going on in her head. She would say that time does not exist; she hoped to transform the past into the present, the present into the future, and the future into past and present. And she would exclaim with a certain hostility: "What are we here for?" Then she would talk about her youth and her childhood. "I am my body, and its light has been shut off," she would murmur. "I have never been anything else, and I never shall be." She would study the shapes of the clouds, believing that what she discerned in them (a jumble of illogical horsemen) meant as much as we did.

When the sky had grown dark, we said goodbye. I watched her as she went away. She did not go up the way she had come, but wandered along the edge of the river, pausing between each step.

RECURRENT DREAMS

His relationships with the world were uncertain. On the other hand, his power of communication with himself was perfect. His inward dialogue moved ahead without interruption.

He was never able to understand why others were not aware that the outside, what one could perceive of animals and objects, was a dream. No one among his friends believed as he did. None of them understood why he had refused to accept the legacy his father had left him at the time of his death, or why he had gone to live in the poverty-stricken hut at the bottom of the ravine.

At first, his brothers and a few of his friends would go down to see him, but as the years passed, no one at all visited him.

His food was the fruit he gathered under the trees, and he drank the water of the river. He passed his days going up and down along the edge of the stream, and when there was no rain he slept lying on the sand. With the passage of time his complexion had changed. His body had taken on an infantile, feminine quality, and there was a pristine brilliance in his eyes.

II

Yet he had gone back to live in the town.

To celebrate his return, one of his brothers gave a dinner. After they had eaten, someone asked him why he had decided to come back. His face remained imperturbable. "I had some dreams," he began. "They kept coming back, night after night, until they convinced me. I dreamed I was in this house (it was the house of his parents), in the living room, leaning against the mantelpiece. I was reading an enormous book. As I turned over a page I would find that the letters were mixed up, as if they had been printed by chance. I would go back to the preceding page and find that the sentences and paragraphs I had just read had already disintegrated. I felt dizzy. Then I heard a voice that seemed to come from behind the flames. I stayed looking straight at the fire, and although I was sweating, I moved nearer to it. Then I heard the voice from behind me. I turned, and was surrounded by fire. The voice came close to me and asked: 'What are you doing here?' 'I'm looking for what is real,' I answered, not wanting to say it. And the voice became a hideous laugh. Then I woke up. And I went on having the dream until I left the hut."

We had listened carefully, but no one spoke. "You don't believe me," he said. He gazed at us, looking for a reaction on our part. "I believe you," I told him. "Why shouldn't I believe you?" "Nobody believes in dreams. For most people it's as though they didn't exist," he explained. He was looking at me with his eyes half shut. "But you seem to understand.

Come." He took my hand, and we went into the adjoining room. He shut the door and led me down a long passageway. Before we got to the living room we could hear the sound of the fire. We sat down among the cushions and he asked me to look at the flames. Then he got up and brought an old, very heavy book which he placed on my lap. "This is the book," he said. "I'll leave you alone so you can glance through it. If you need anything, call me." The sound of the door being shut seemed disproportionately loud. I opened the book at random. The page was blank. I turned it: the next page was also blank. The fire had gone out. I called several times but he did not answer. I leaned back against the pillows and shut my eyes.

I dreamed that the voice of a woman was telling me that for me things would be different. I opened my eyes: I was in a cobbled alley. The melodious voice was at my back. "Come, this way." I continued, and we went through a very narrow door into a room without furnishings or windows. She pushed me into the middle of the room and shut the door. "If you want to get into heaven, you must know yourself, and if you want to know yourself, you must live here for a while," she explained in a firm voice.

A week later I was selling my belongings and taking no notice of the world.

A VERSION OF MY DEATH

I

I don't know who I was writing to. I let the pen fall onto the table in front of me.

I ran downstairs.

A little later I went back and dropped onto my mattress. It is on the floor.

II

They found me today.

I was in my room. Asleep.

There were four of them; they came enveloped in a dream, (the four dressed in blue and red.)

One of them, the tallest, took out a paper and read, while the others watched.

The short wrinkled one came up to me from behind.

With his damp hands he touched my back. I could not move.

In silence they left.

When I awoke it was still night.

The next day I did not go out of the house. In vain I waited for them to return. Almost without moving.

III

I did not go out for seven days.
I am plumper and I see more clearly.
I think they have forgotten me.

IV

My house has only one room. There is only one door.
I cannot hide in it.
Perhaps they have forgiven me.

V

I am not afraid. Not in any part of me.
The light that comes in through one of the two windows is clean.
It shines on the dust that already covers everything in
the house.

VI

The roofbeams are still young.
The light — the light is blue.
There is knocking at the door. I do not open it.
It was the wind.
No. They have not forgotten me.

VII

Now I see: it was an oversight.

I keep the letter in which they announce my death.

It is on the floor beside my bed.

The letter does not say when. Nevertheless it gives a description of the day.

There is a great amount of light and the clouds are almost red.

Below, the earth, soft and green. The silence is unbroken.

They describe my face: my eyes are open and my lips lightly touch the ground.

I seem to have read those lines before. Many years ago. The clouds and the moon were the same, but the ground was stone. Like ice.

And the lines described a mouth that was thirsty and dead.

VIII

Today is not hot, but the air is dry.

The girl who brings the milk and eggs has not come.

THE ANIMAL

When he woke from sleep, his eyes were already open. For an instant he failed to recognize his wife, who was looking at him. He did not mention the fact to her, and shut his eyes. "You were dreaming?" she wanted to know. He had been, but the dream was forgotten. In its stead, he recalled a nightmare from his childhood.

In this he had dreamed of a kind of animal the like of which he had never seen; its ghastly face was his own, weak and sad, and bleeding slowly at the mouth. Its body was formless and gleamed like gold. They were together in the bed, which in the dream had grown to immense proportions. The animal breathed painfully, as if the air around it were insufficient for it. At length he asked it: "Who are you?" It shrugged, groaned, and did not reply. It was then that he had felt the dream's horror, and had awakened. There had been tears on his cheeks, and this made him think that he was still dreaming. "I'm asleep," he had told himself. "When I wake up, I'll be the animal."

He opened his eyes and looked out of the window: a very high red building with scores of black windows. He turned to his wife, and she looked at him. In her pupils he saw the deformed image of his mouth, and he turned back to stare at the window. He felt like saying something, but he did not know what. A fine, invisible rain came down, and the sound of the traffic moving on the avenue grew louder.

UNCERTAIN READINGS

I

My older brother died a year ago today.

I was in the back garden cutting the weeds that were growing up around the flame trees that he had planted as a boy.

The doorbell began to ring. I ran, crossing through the house, but the door opened before I could reach it.

"It was open," he explained, "and I took the liberty . . ."

He wore a grey wool overcoat and black shoes. His hair hung down to his shoulders, and he looked at me as he always had. Shutting his eyes slightly, and with a suave smile.

I confess that he inspired me, if not with fear, with something like it. From my upper thighs it rose to my stomach, threatening to make me release my bladder. It continued to rise, until it fell feebly out through my throat.

"What can I offer you?"

For reply he put a slow hand between his chest and his coat, without looking away.

He took out a white envelope and held it out to me.

Before I could take it he put it back into his pocket. He turned and began to walk away.

I could not help it. Suddenly I found myself following him.

I saw my feet moving, one after the other, in the black shoes. Afterward I saw the overcoat. I stopped and went back to the house. The door was ajar. I pushed it and found myself facing a young man, his hands dark with earth and his lips stiff with fear.

II

He had to take longer steps in order to catch up with me.

"Wait," he said.

Without turning to look at him, I imagined his eyes, and slowed my gait.

He did not stop talking during the rest of the walk, and I looked straight ahead, so as not to see him.

He spoke about the life of a certain man. About his parents and some of his friends. When we said good-bye, he called me by the man's name.

"So long," he said, and he laughed as he went away.

When I got home it was clear that someone had been there without my permission.

When I left it, the house had been empty except for the mattress, the small radio and the stove.

A curtain has been hung over the window and a rug now covers the floor. On the rug there is a long table of a dark wood, and the table is set for three, including a bottle of wine.

I lay down on the mattress. A woman with green eyes and bright red lips, followed by a youth with very black hair, came soundlessly through the doorway.

They sat down at the table, acting as though they had not seen me.

They talk and laugh, but I am unable to understand them. I rise and sit down at the table, although I am not hungry. Then I stretch out my hand to reach for the crystal carafe containing the wine, but my hand goes through it.

They look at me with serious expressions. I notice that her hair is as dark as the young man's.

I get up and lie down once more on the mattress, and behave as though I had not seen them.

After they had eaten they packed up everything they had brought, from the curtain to the wine. And they went away. "So long," the two said as one, and they softly shut the door.

III

That afternoon I flew back to the city where I was born.

There was someone waiting for me. I greeted him warmly, and noticed that he saw himself reflected in me, because he glanced at me in the same way as I glance into the mirror.

Quickly I got together my things and flew out of the city.

The following day I went out shopping with a woman.

She was in front of a huge mirror (which swallows the whole shop), trying on a red dress which, instead of covering her, made it possible to see the inside of her body through her skin.

A loud noise approaches, bouncing from one wall to the other. It comes in through the window, shattering it.

I cover my head with my hands.

The broken window goes through the mirror and what there is inside it.

People are running. It is late and the sun is red.

We are all running and shouting.

The air is full of open eyes and small round pieces of iron.

I feel a strange heat in my head, like the heat felt while urinating.

I go back to meet her; she is still wearing the red dress. We climb into an ancient carriage and drive away down a road paved with white stones. Underneath the road there is a river.

It is early. Almost morning.

The milkmaid came earlier that morning.

She could not tell me what had happened.

She did not tell me that she had seen me before, many times.

That she had already touched me.

We looked at each other until neither one could see the other.

Her hands go inside my clothes and tear them.

Her odor sticks to my skin.

My arms turn red and her neck grows soft.

Her eyes go inside mine, and my eyes stare at her skin.

They came for me yesterday.

They took me to a room full of men.

From the other side of the wall comes the sound of women's voices.

"They say the ones who are there are all dead."

In the morning they gather up our trash, our leftover food and dirty water.

Every three days they take away one of us, bringing him back three days later with a different face, but wearing the same clothes.

They say that once you are outside you no longer remember having been here.

The voices of the women are the only relief.

They filter through the wall and float among us. Between our fingers and legs, warming them.

Sometimes they go in through the ears and enter the head. Then one suffers.

A PRISONER

The first dream was very short: three angels were assuring him that God is not God. On awakening, he did not recognize the sounds coming up from the valley; he did not know where he was. He looked at the bare dusty floor. He looked at the window and shut his eyes. A late afternoon sun, a forest, a dry root in a wall, a mountain and a river. He saw all this, his eyes closed, before the second dream. Suddenly there was blood in the water of the river; the dream was starting.

He hears tiny voices going downstream. He dreams that his body is floating in the river. Four or six arms drag him to the shore and leave him stretched out on the pebbles. He stands up. There is a high mountain. At the top, between the moving trees, the moon is rising. With an ingenuous optimism he fails to remember that he is dreaming. He kneels; carefully he clasps his hands in front of him, and shuts his eyes. When he opens them once more, the mountain looks fainter, almost inacessible. He presses on it lightly with his foot; then he begins to climb. On the way to the top, twice he sees the lazy shadow of an animal crossing the path. A falcon makes circles against the sky, and he remembers the moon several times. When he gets to the summit, wind veils the light; a fine rain starts to fall, and it grows dark. In front of him on a rock, a stone statue sits looking into the distance. The rain stops, the clouds move away, and the gigantic moon reappears. The man thinks: "It doesn't matter what becomes of me," and recalls with some surprise the voices which told him that God is not God. The song of the river comes up from the valley. He takes a last glance at the face of the stone image, backs up a few steps, and slowly turns around. Then it is as if someone were slashing his back, and he awakens. Beside him a man lies sleeping; his body gives off a strong odor.

A drop of water lands on his forehead, he hears the distant report of a gun, the whistling of a bullet, and he imagines its course through the night. He hears the low barking of dogs, and voices.

The third dream was stranger. When the murmur of the useless shot had died away, he closed his eyes and went directly into the dream. He saw nothing but a light, a heavy, weakening light. There was a voice, but he did not understand what it was trying to tell him. Still in his dream, he said to himself: "I'm dreaming that I'm God," and he remembered that he was sleeping in a gully and that he was a prisoner. He opened his eyes and saw the rose-colored shadows of the trees. It was growing light.

THE BLACK ROOM

His life was spent alone with his sister in a building which no longer exists. He was convinced that the door into the street was the opening to a tunnel which he refused to enter. It was enough for him to walk from one wall to another in his rectangular room, with the aid of a staff that he waved to and fro. Some nights he awoke with his arms outstretched as if to protect his face, or to touch something which he felt was in front of him. These occasions troubled him. Nearby was his sister, who would touch him in order to calm him.

All that he knew about the world he had gathered from what she had told him. She would read to him, and she had taken his hands in hers and made him touch the edge of the table. She had slid them over the surfaces of other objects so he could feel their qualities. Although he had no concept of its actual appearance, with the passage of time the room had become a compact and well-defined world. Intuitively he knew the form of his universe: he surmised the existence of the squalid floor, the kitchen, the dark pots, the window, the windows across the street.

THE SEEING EYE

I admit that I envied him. With his skin like
metal, his hair so black that it seemed blue, his soft
empty gaze, he fitted my concept of a man who has
made contact with God.

The first time I felt the impulse to blind myself,
six or seven years ago, we were in a crowd, strolling
arm in arm. It was the end of the rainy season. I remember the moment vividly: the grey and yellow
afternoon, the sunlight wandering along the edge of
the river, the sharp voices of the children, and, suddenly, desire, the desire to be equal to him, to look
into the darkness and *see* it always.

Two or three months later I took him for a drive
in his car. We were moving in a straight line; the road
went on and on, not turning one way or the other,
toward the horizon. Without looking at it, he seemed
to be watching the sky: there were a few solitary
clouds, almost imperceptible. No thought, no memory crossed my mind; there was neither tree, nor
rock, nor wall in the landscape. On our right the
sun was about to set, and the sky had turned red and
iron grey. There was no wind; the car rushed ahead at
unvarying speed. I shut my eyes, had a sensation of
freedom, opened them again. Ahead, far off, I saw a
mountain. I shut my eyes again. I was aware of the
dull sound of the tires on the paved road, I felt a

trembling in my thighs and belly, and repressed the impulse to raise my eyelids. It was then, with my eyes still closed, that I saw I was enveloped in a gold-colored cloud, heavy but luminous and transparent. I wanted to be blind, and I said to myself in silence, in a voice that was not mine: "If only I could be like this." I opened my eyes and looked at him; he smiled. I thought—and I still wonder—"Is it possible that he doesn't know what is happening?" It was now dark. The headlights lit up the road; we went along in silence. When we reached the mountain the curves and windings began.

I used to go to his room each night to read aloud to him. That night when I went there I did not find him. I hoped to talk with him about what I had felt. I searched through the entire house, but did not find him. From outside I heard the croaking of frogs. Nausea, heaviness, a sad, penetrating fatigue. I went back downstairs to the sitting-room. On the lowest step lay a battered old paintbrush. Above the mantelpiece there hung a medal in the form of a six-pointed star. I took it down, and I remember, and shall always remember, that it trembled in my hand. I went out into the garden. The clouds were heavy with rain. I went to the stone bench near the fountain and sat down. For the last time I saw the night. I moved my eyelids, and with the sharp edge of the star I slashed my eyes. There was no pain. I seemed to be falling; a tepid current ran down my cheeks. I moved my hands in front of my face and did not see them. From behind me I heard him calling out to me.

(I am not astonished by the solitude or the darkness there is in the air, and much less by the thought that I am in a hell of my own creation. Sometimes my past surprises me, and the memory I have of his voice.)

Printed in the USA
CPSIA information can be obtained
at www.ICGtesting.com
JSHW082222140824
68134JS00015B/691

9 780872 861640